W9-BGQ-988

Disney
Pooh's
Grand Adventure
The Search for Christopher Robin

Bruce Talkington Illustrated by John Kurtz

SCHOLASTIC INC.

New York Toronto London Auckland Sydney

Based on the Pooh stories by A. A. Milne (copyright The Pooh Properties Trust).

No part of this publication may be reproduced in whole or in part, or stored in a retrieval system, or transmitted in any form or by any means, electronic, mechanical, photocopying, recording, or otherwise, without written permission of the publisher. For information regarding permission, write to Disney Press, 114 Fifth Avenue, New York, NY 10011-5690.

ISBN 0-590-12811-6

Copyright © 1997 by Disney Enterprises, Inc. All rights reserved. Published by Scholastic Inc., 555 Broadway, New York, NY 10012, by arrangement with Disney Press. SCHOLASTIC and associated logos are trademarks and/or registered trademarks of Scholastic Inc.

12 11 10 9 8 7 6 5 4 3 2   7 8 9/9 0 1 2/0

Printed in the U.S.A.

First Scholastic printing, September 1997

Disney

Pooh's Grand Adventure

The Search for Christopher Robin

It seemed like any other sparkling, fresh, golden, end-of-the-summer day in the Hundred-Acre Wood. If something out of the ordinary were about to happen, Winnie the Pooh was unaware of it. Pooh was, in fact, pretty much unaware of everything except what he'd had for breakfast and how long it was till lunch.

He did know that it was time to meet his very best friend, Christopher Robin, on their enchanted hill for another day of being "we" rather than simply Pooh and Christopher Robin.

But today Christopher Robin's usually happy smile had somehow turned upside down and pulled his face into a worried frown.

"Pooh Bear," Christopher Robin sighed. "There's something I have to tell you."

"This isn't a time for telling," said Pooh in reply. He clutched Christopher Robin's hand tightly and tried to run his tumbly run. "It's a time for doing!" exclaimed Pooh.

"Doing what?" Christopher Robin wanted to know.

"Oh, any old thing," answered Pooh. "As long as we do it together."

"Suppose," said Christopher Robin, not looking Pooh in the eye, "suppose a tomorrow came and we weren't together?"

Pooh tugged on an ear in hopes that that would make Christopher Robin's question easier to understand.

"What does 'not together' mean?" he asked.

"It means I will always be with you," Christopher Robin assured his friend, "but that I might not always be here."

"Then I'm glad it's tomorrow," smiled Pooh, "because then I don't have to think about it today."

"Silly old bear," said Christopher Robin.

The next morning, however, when Pooh arrived at the hill, there was not a sign of Christopher Robin anywhere. That was one surprise.

And there was another one as well.

Sitting in the middle of the clearing was a large pot of honey! It was wrapped in a brightly colored ribbon and bow. And attached to the ribbon was a note in a very neat handwriting.

"Oh," said Pooh at the sight of the note.

Rumble, said Pooh's tummy at the sight of the honey.

"My head says this honey might not be for me," sighed Pooh. "However, my tummy is certain that it can't possibly belong to anyone else.

"I'll simply have to see which one my friends agree with," decided Pooh with another, even larger, sigh.

"I was hoping, sort of," explained Pooh later to his friends when they'd joined him on the enchanted hill, "that this large smackeral of something sweet was for me."

"Why don't you read the note and find out?" suggested Rabbit.

"Yes," agreed Pooh, scratching his head and wrinkling his brow. "That sounds like the thing to do all right. But," he said hopefully, "perhaps one of you would care to read it first?"

Rabbit, Tigger, Piglet, and Eeyore exchanged skeptical looks.

"Maybe we should let Owl read it," rumbled Eeyore. "If reading it is what you really want."

"Yes!" responded Pooh, greatly relieved.

And so Owl read the mysterious note.

"Christopher Robin," announced Owl, "has gone to *Skull*!"

"*Skull?!*" gasped Tigger. "Are you absoposilutely sure an' certain?"

"Well," admitted Owl, "what else can S-C-H-O-O-L spell?"

"You got me there, featherhead," sighed Tigger. "Sure sounds terrifryin', don't it?"

Pooh, looking extremely determined for a Bear of Very Little Brain, smacked his fist into his paw.

"We must get Christopher Robin back," he said. "To here! And us! And *me*!"

"Then it's a *quest*," hooted Owl in delight, and immediately began to prepare for the expedition, supplying his friends with a wonderfully impressive-looking map that no one could read.

In what seemed no time at all, the rescue party was crossing the bridge into the deepest and darkest part of the Hundred-Acre Wood as Owl waved an enthusiastic farewell.

"Good luck! Toodle-oo!" he called cheerily. "I'll keep a sharp eye out for your return . . . *if* you do return, of course."

"Saying good-bye to Owl is making me nervous," said Piglet.

"Not as nervous as sayin' hello to that Skullasaurus is going to make you," sniffed Tigger.

"*Skullasaurus!*" exclaimed Pooh, Rabbit, Eeyore, and Piglet in frightened unison.

"Wha-what Skullasaurus?" demanded Rabbit.

"Why, the one at Skull," laughed Tigger. "You wouldn't call a place Skull if there wasn't a Skullasaurus there, would ya?"

No one had an answer for that question, so they began their trek, all trying to look in every direction at once.

It was—as Tigger described it later—"A horribibble trip!"

Their prickly
tramp through the
Forest of Thorns,
painful as it turned out
to be, at least "pointed"
them in the right
direction.

Tromping through
the Valley of Flowers was
a great relief until their
very small companion was
Piglet-napped by a horde
of overly affectionate
Flutterbys!

By the time Piglet was rescued, the map had been lost, they had crossed the Screaming Gorge on a very uncooperative log bridge, the map had been found again, and they had survived the Valley of Mists.

They all ended up standing before the entrance of the looming Skull Cave feeling rather out of sorts. Everyone was ready for a rescue party to come and save them. But they knew one wasn't coming because the only rescue party in the Hundred-Acre Wood was them! And they were already there.

Once they'd entered the deep, dank, and dingy darkness of Skull
Cave, the growling began!

"The Skullasaurus!" squeaked Piglet.

"And it's gettin' closer," moaned Eeyore.

Another low growl erupted from the darkness.

"And hungrier!" gulped Tigger.

In order to find Christopher Robin as quickly as possible (as well as to make it difficult for the Skullasaurus to find them), the rescue party split up. They rushed off to search in different directions.

However, all they found was each other in the Crystal Cavern. Not a hint of Christopher Robin was uncovered. And it was discovered that Pooh Bear was missing, too!

Then, the growls got louder and louder, and everyone was certain Pooh had been snatched by the lurking Skullasaurus!

"I'm going to miss that bear," sniffed Tigger, as they all wiped their eyes and blew their noses noisily. "He was a great guy in a snowball fight. Couldn't throw worth banana skins, but, boy, was he a swell target!"

Thankfully, before they'd had the opportunity to miss Pooh Bear for more than the briefest instant, they found him again! And they found the growl, too. Louder than ever!

The growls grew more and more fierce, and a shadow suddenly loomed over the rescue party! "This is it!" Rabbit squawked. "It's . . . it's . . . !"

They all held their breath, but before Rabbit could finish, the
shadow walked into the light and revealed itself to be . . .
Christopher Robin!

After Pooh and the others had swarmed over him with hugs,
handshakes, and "Hoo-hoo-hoos" of relief, Christopher Robin had a
question.

"What are you all doing here?" he asked.

"Why, that's oblivious!" chuckled Tigger.

"Yes," agreed Pooh. "We're here to save you from Skull," he informed Christopher Robin proudly.

"Skull?" responded Christopher Robin. "I was at *school*."

"That Owl," said Tigger in exasperation. "I *knew* skull had another Y in it."

"But . . . but . . . what about the Skullasaurus?" squeaked Piglet. "We hear him!"

As if responding to its name, another growl filled the cave!

"There it is again," shouted Piglet, as he jumped into Pooh's arms.

"That's no Skullasaurus," Christopher Robin informed them with a chuckle. "That's the sound of the rumbly-tumbly tummy of a hungry-for-honey bear."

Christopher Robin poked Pooh gently in his middle and the growl sounded again, not at all scary now that they saw where it came from.

Later, when everyone had eaten and said, "Thank you," and, "You're very welcome," and, "Come again soon," Christopher Robin and Pooh went to sit together atop the Grassy Knoll.

"Pooh?" said Christopher Robin after a long silence that was full to the brim of the two of them simply being together. "Whatever happens, will you come up here sometimes and . . . remember?"

"Remember what?" answered Pooh, without opening his eyes.
"Remember that even if we're apart, I'll always be with you."
Pooh opened his eyes and looked up at his very best friend.
"Yes, Christopher Robin," he said. "And I'll always be with
you, too."

And if, by chance or good fortune, we manage to keep our hearts in the Right Place, these two will always be with us as well!